The Rescue of BUNNY WUNNY

Emma Chichester Clark

HarperCollins *Children's Books*

Bunny Wunny
belonged to Imelda.
He was her favourite
fluffy toy.

He was given to Imelda
when she was a tiny baby.

She **never** let him out of her sight.

No matter how many
brave little toys she had …

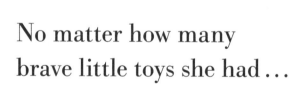

…Bunny Wunny was the one
she always wanted the **most**.

Imelda's parents **adored** her.

She was the **apple** of their eye ...

... the **cherry** on their cherry pie.

They gave her
EVERYTHING
she ever wanted.

And they loved Imelda more than
ANYTHING.

But, sadly, Imelda did not **really** love Bunny Wunny.

She wasn't very kind to him. And there came a day when Bunny Wunny could stand her **no longer**.

He **had** to get **away**.

WHERE'S BUNNY WUNNY?

screamed Imelda.
She nearly yelled
the house down.

Bunny Wunny
shook with fear.

"What's the matter, Angel Pie?"
asked her father.

FIND
BUNNY WUNNY!

screamed Imelda.

So they
searched

high

and

low…

But Bunny Wunny was not coming out for anyone.

"Let's go to the toy shop and buy another rabbit!" said Imelda's mother.

NO! I DON'T WANT ANOTHER ONE!

Imelda yelled.

So Imelda and her parents went to the pet shop. The nice man smiled at Imelda.

"Can I help you?" he asked.

Imelda bared her teeth.

"I WANT A RABBIT!"

Imelda shouted.

All the rabbits hurried
to the back of their pen.

All except one, that is.
It went on quietly eating a carrot…
didn't even look up.

THAT ONE!

cried Imelda.

Back at home, Imelda sat in her room and **stared** at the rabbit.

She **poked** it with her finger but he didn't even turn round.

she said.

You're making a BIG mistake!

replied the rabbit.

Imelda's eyes opened wide.

The rabbit was suddenly the size of a **poodle**.

Imelda blinked.

Then the rabbit was suddenly as big as Imelda.

Imelda gasped.

And then the rabbit was **as tall as her father.**

Imelda screamed.

Quiet, monster! It's time to teach you a lesson!

said the rabbit.

Imelda's parents
popped their heads
round the door.

"Good grief!"
said her father.

Please,
join us!

said the rabbit.

"We need to talk about Imelda."

Imelda **snorted** like a warthog.

"That's **our** darling!"
said Imelda's mother.

"Our *dearest* darling!"
said her father.

You mean ...
you *like* the way
she behaves?

asked the rabbit.

"Like her? We *adore* everything
about her!" said Imelda's parents.

"We love her just the way she is," said Imelda's mother.

The rabbit was quite lost for words.

Well, I can see my help isn't needed here,

said the rabbit.

You can help me!

squeaked
a little voice.
And out hopped
Bunny Wunny.

RRRRRRRAAAAAAARRR!

roared Imelda.

Bye, Imelda!
Au revoir, arrivederci!
So long...

called Bunny Wunny.

Are you sure
you don't want
to be kinder
to your toys,
Imelda?

asked the rabbit.

But Imelda
said nothing.

"Some people will never change,"
said the rabbit.

"No," agreed Bunny Wunny.
"It's a shame it's not a happy ending."

"I'm happy!" said the rabbit.

"Me too," said Bunny Wunny.

But what about Imelda?

Who cares?

said the rabbit.